Mr. Putter and Tabby Pour the Tea

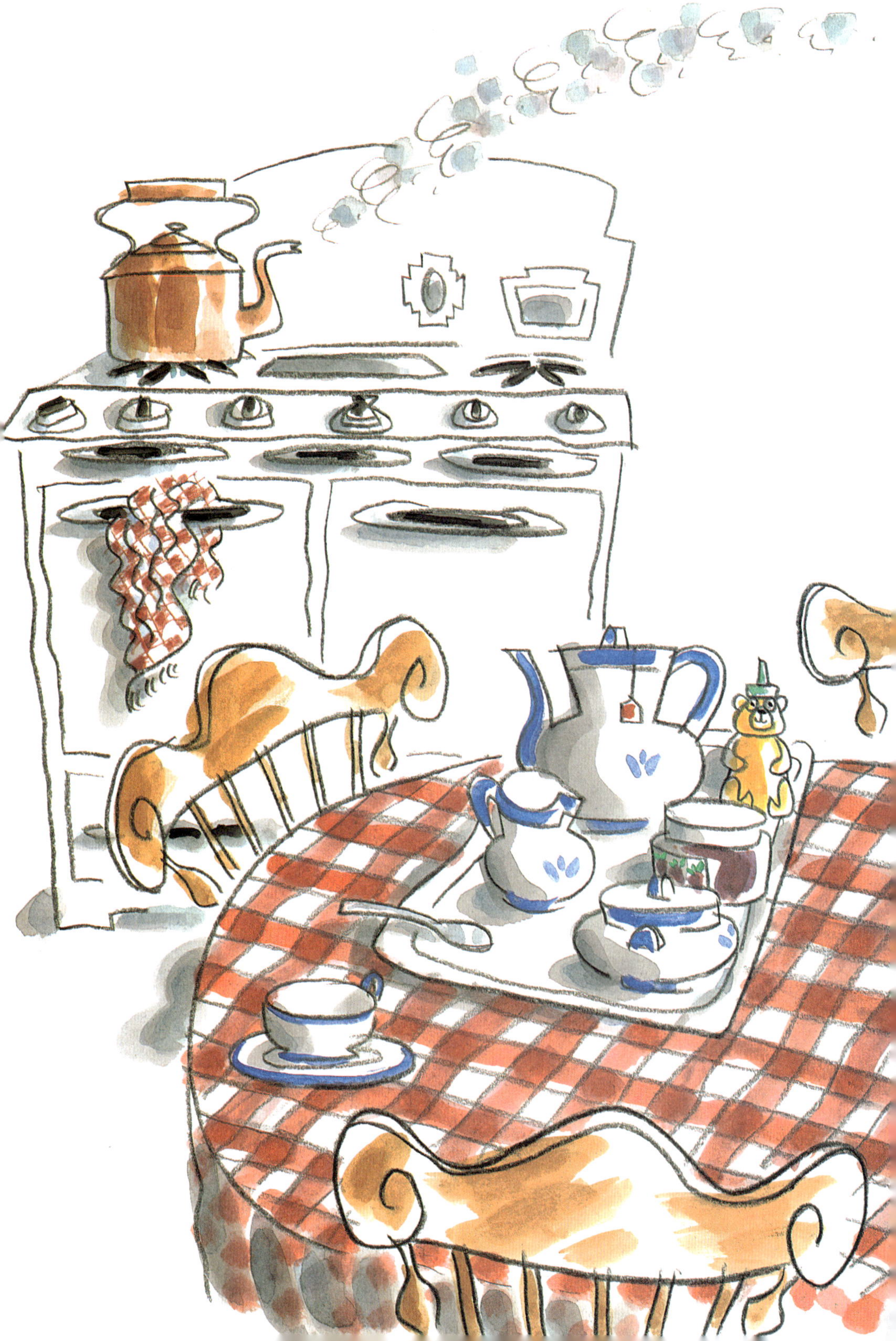

CYNTHIA RYLANT

Mr. Putter and Tabby Pour the Tea

Illustrated by
ARTHUR HOWARD

Scholastic Inc.
New York   Toronto   London   Auckland   Sydney

For Grandmama and Whiskers
—C. R.

For James Tilton
—A. H.

No part of this publication may be reproduced in whole or in part, or stored in a retrieval system, or transmitted in any form or by any means, electronic, mechanical, photocopying, recording, or otherwise, without written permission of the publisher. For information regarding permission, write to Permissions Department, Harcourt Brace & Company, 8th Floor, Orlando, FL 32887.

ISBN 0-590-25953-9

Text copyright © 1994 by Cynthia Rylant.
Illustrations copyright © 1994 by Arthur Howard. All rights reserved.
Published by Scholastic Inc., 555 Broadway, New York, NY 10012,
by arrangement with Harcourt Brace & Company.

12 11 10 9 8 7 6 5 4 3 2   5 6 7 8 9/9 0/0

Printed in the U.S.A.   23

First Scholastic printing, March 1995

1
Mr. Putter

2
Tabby

3
Mr. Putter and Tabby

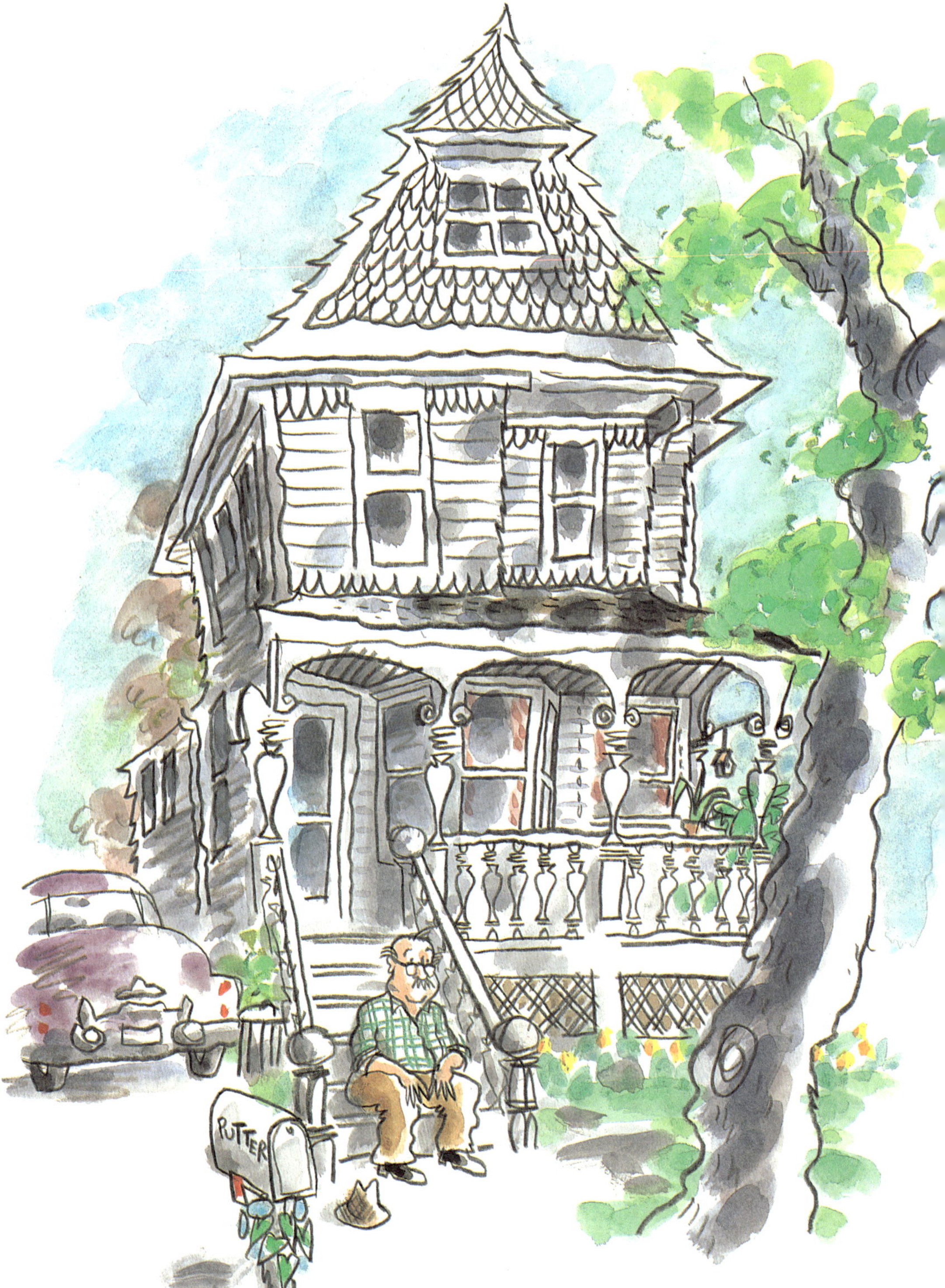
PUTTER

1
Mr. Putter

Before he got his fine cat, Tabby,
Mr. Putter lived all alone.

In the mornings he had no one
to share his English muffins.
In the afternoons he had no one
to share his tea.

And in the evenings there was no one Mr. Putter could tell his stories to. And he had the most wonderful stories to tell.

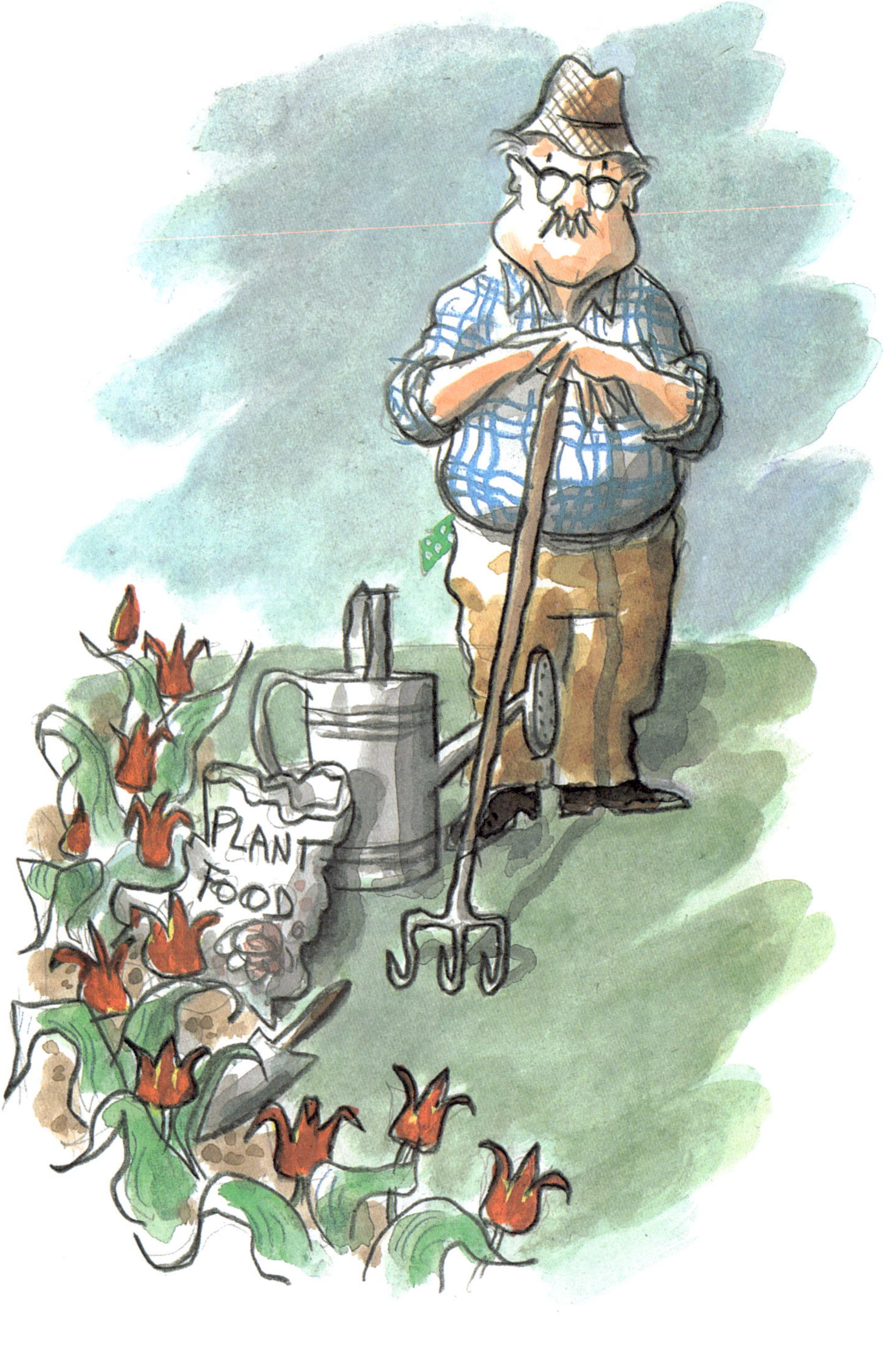
PLANT FOOD

All day long as Mr. Putter
clipped his roses
and fed his tulips
and watered his trees,
Mr. Putter wished for
some company.

He had warm muffins to eat.

He had good tea to pour.

And he had wonderful stories to tell.

Mr. Putter was tired of living alone.

Mr. Putter wanted a cat.

2
Tabby

Mr. Putter went to the pet store.
"Do you have cats?" he asked the
pet store lady.
"We have fourteen," she said.
Mr. Putter was delighted.
But when he looked into the cage,
he was not.

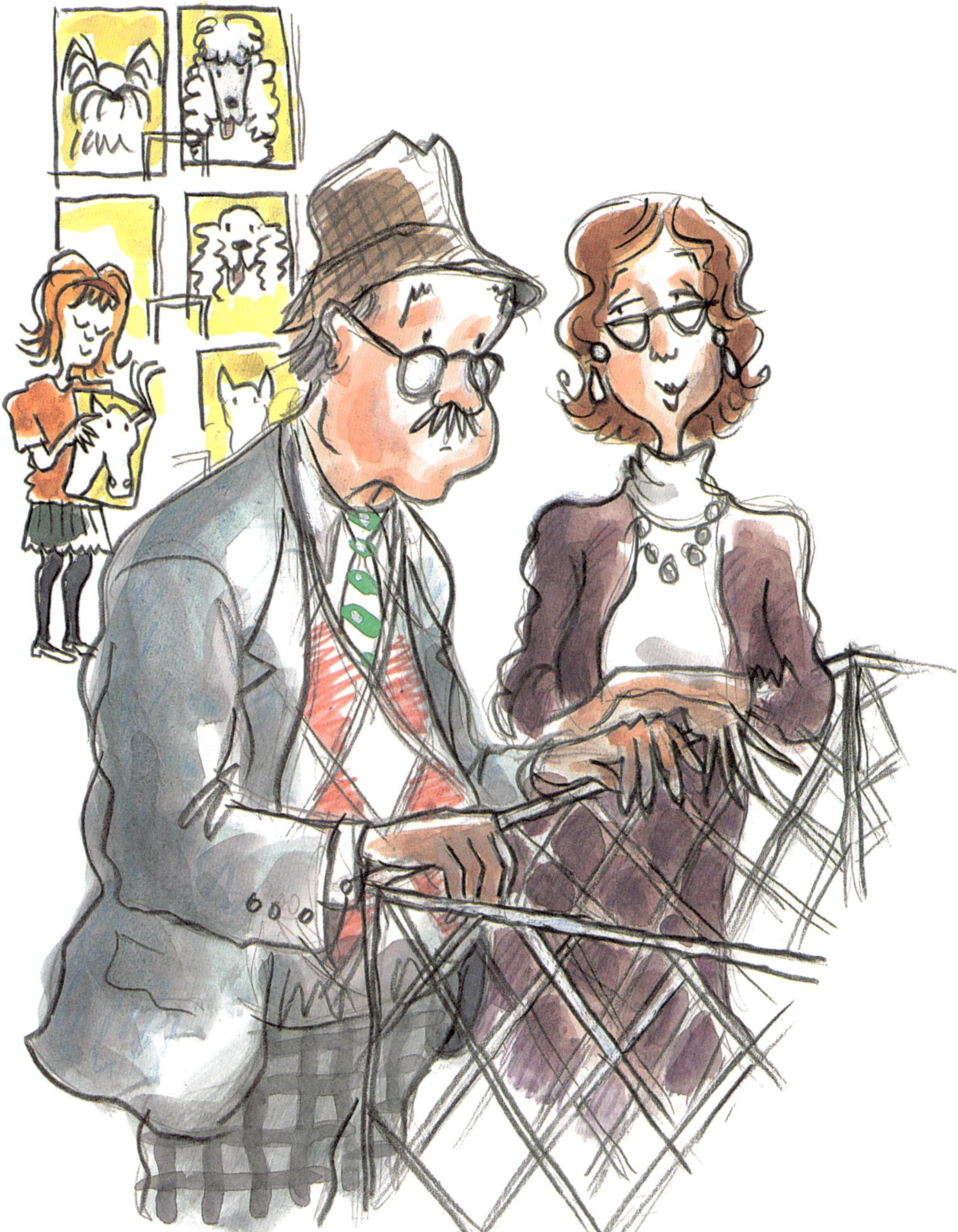

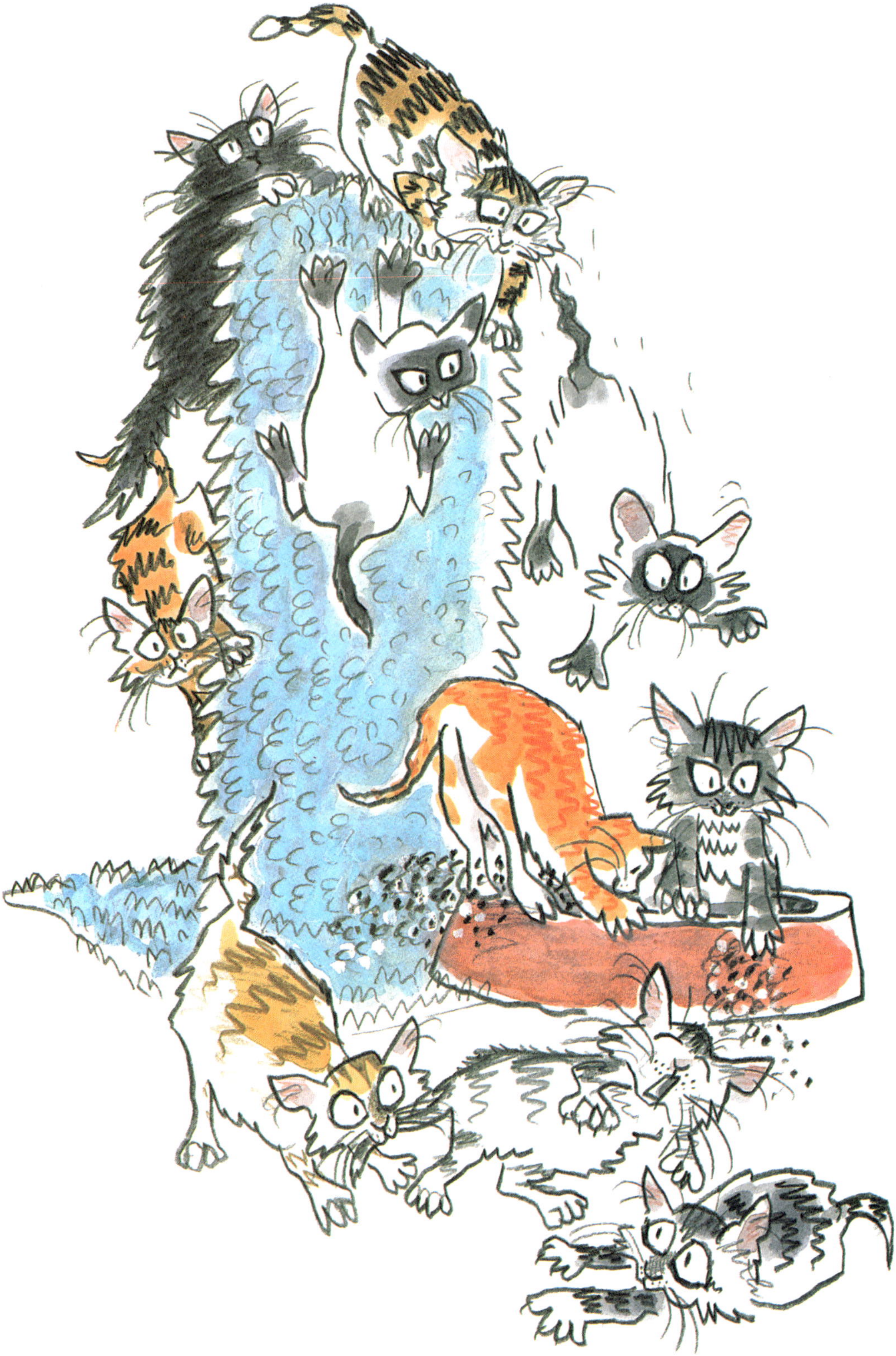

"These are kittens," he said.
"I was hoping for a cat."
"Oh, no one wants cats, sir,"
said the pet store lady.
"They are not cute.
They are not peppy."

Mr. Putter himself had not been cute and peppy for a very long time.

He said, "I want a cat."

"Then go to the shelter, sir,"
said the pet store lady.
"You are sure to find a cat."

Mr. Putter went to the shelter.

"Have you any cats?"
he asked the shelter man.
"We have a fat gray one,
a thin black one,
and an old yellow one," said the man.
"Did you say old?" asked Mr. Putter.

The shelter man brought Mr. Putter
the old yellow cat.
Its bones creaked,
its fur was thinning,
and it seemed a little deaf.
Mr. Putter creaked,
his hair was thinning,
and he was a little deaf, too.

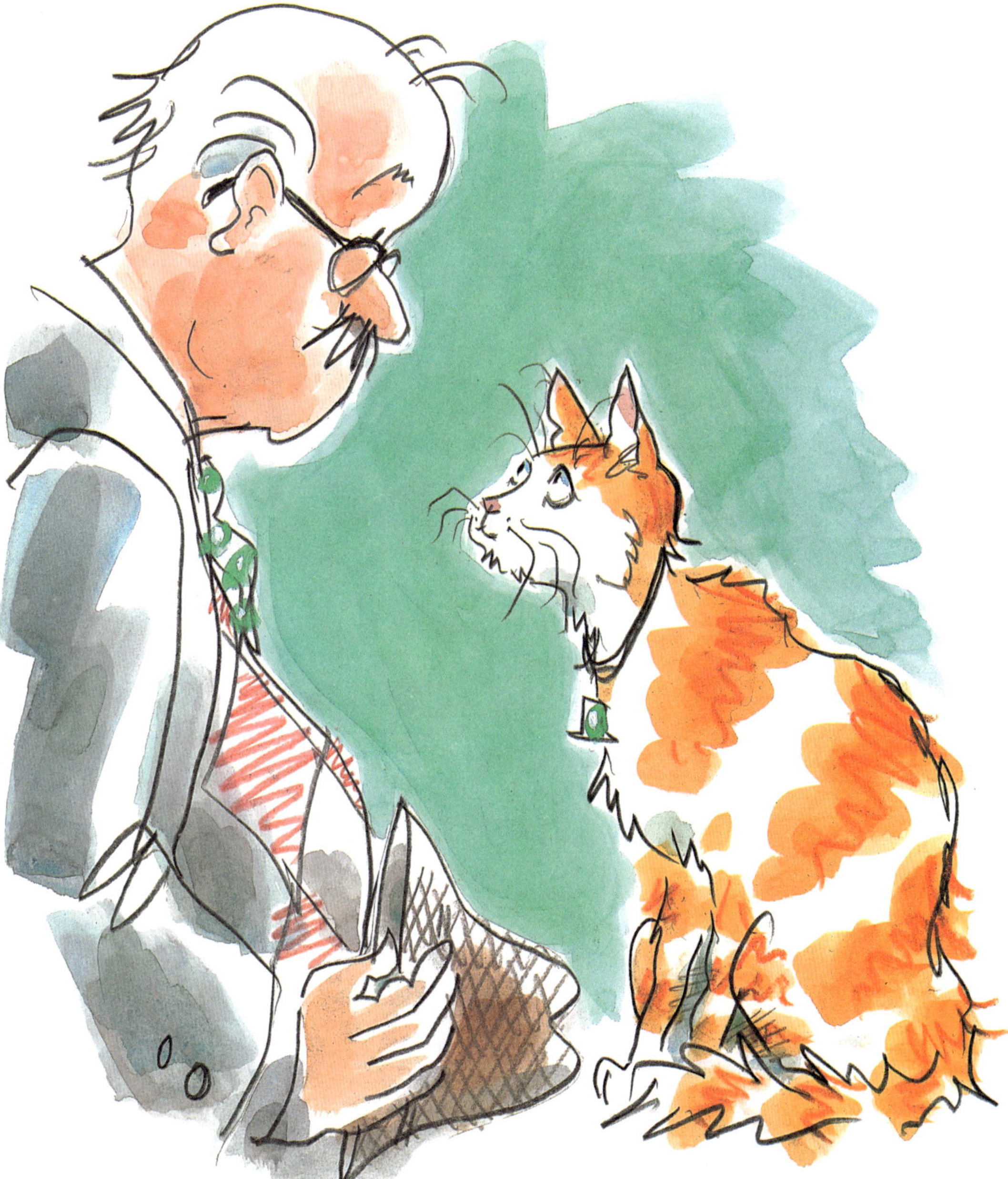

So he took the old yellow cat home.

He named her Tabby.

And that is how their life began.

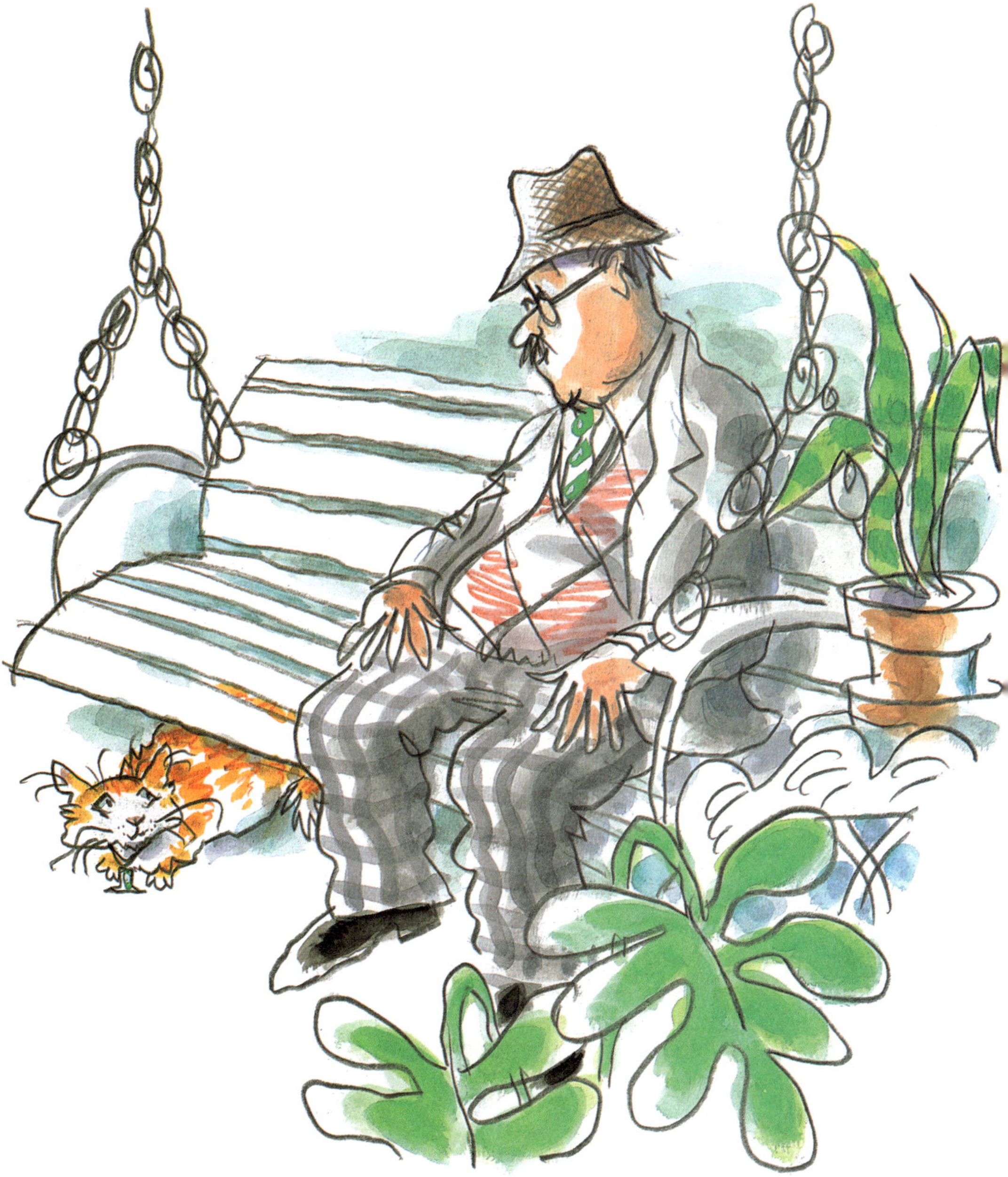

3
Mr. Putter and Tabby

Tabby loved Mr. Putter's tulips.
She was old,
and beautiful things
meant more to her.

She would rub past all
the yellow tulips.
Then she would roll past
all the red tulips.

Then she would take her bath
among all the pink tulips.
Mr. Putter clipped roses
while Tabby bathed.

In the mornings
Mr. Putter and Tabby liked to share
an English muffin.
Mr. Putter ate his with jam.
Tabby ate hers with cream cheese.

In the afternoons
Mr. Putter and Tabby
liked to share tea.
Mr. Putter took his with sugar.
Tabby took hers with cream.

And in the evenings
they sat by the window,
and Mr. Putter told stories.
He told the most wonderful stories.
Each story made Tabby purr.

On summer days they warmed their
old bones together in the sun.
On fall days they took
long walks through the trees.
And on winter days they turned
the opera up *very* loud.

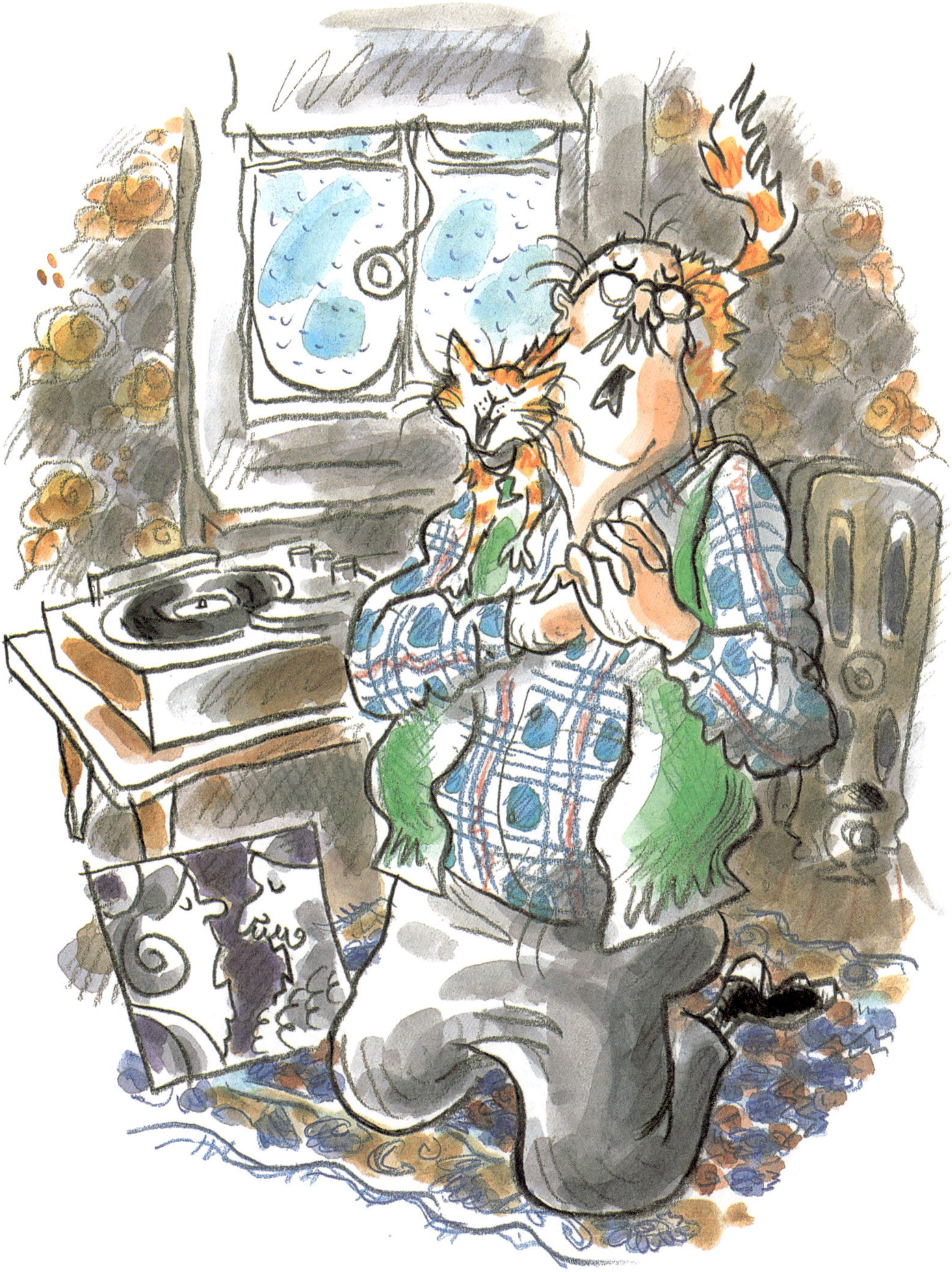

After a while it seemed as if
they had always lived together.
Tabby knew just what Mr. Putter
was going to do next.
Mr. Putter knew just where Tabby
was going to sleep next.

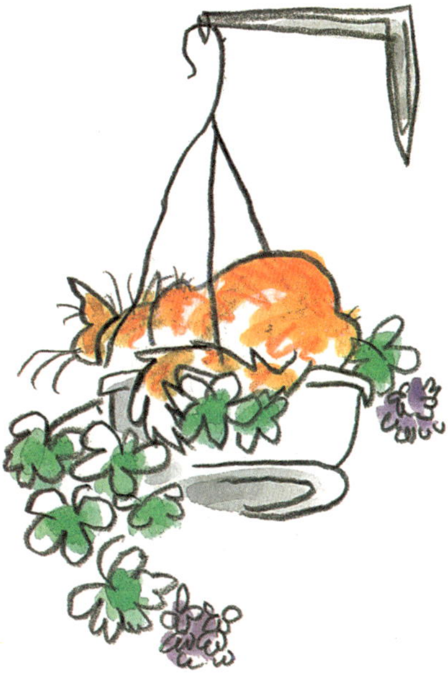

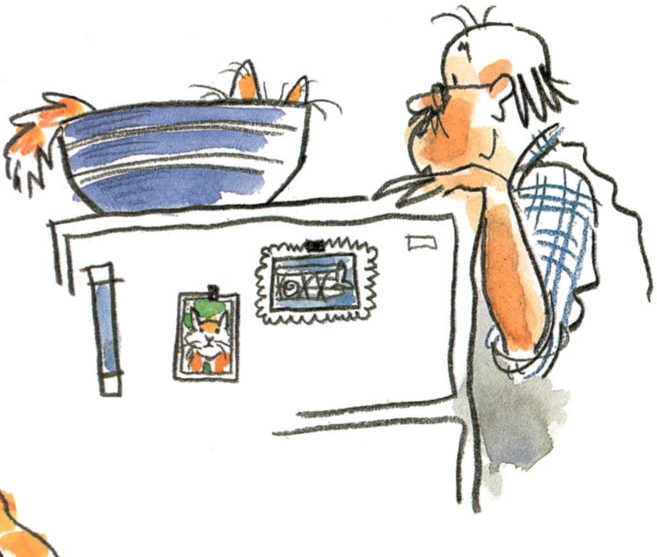

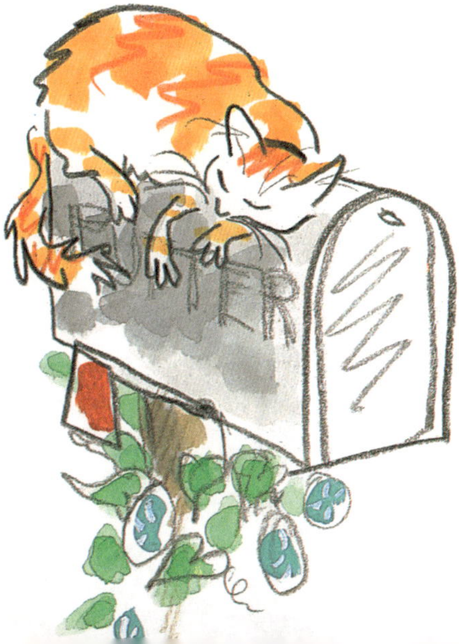

In the mornings each looked for the other as soon as they opened their eyes.

And at night each looked for
the other as their eyes were closing.
Mr. Putter could not remember
life without Tabby.

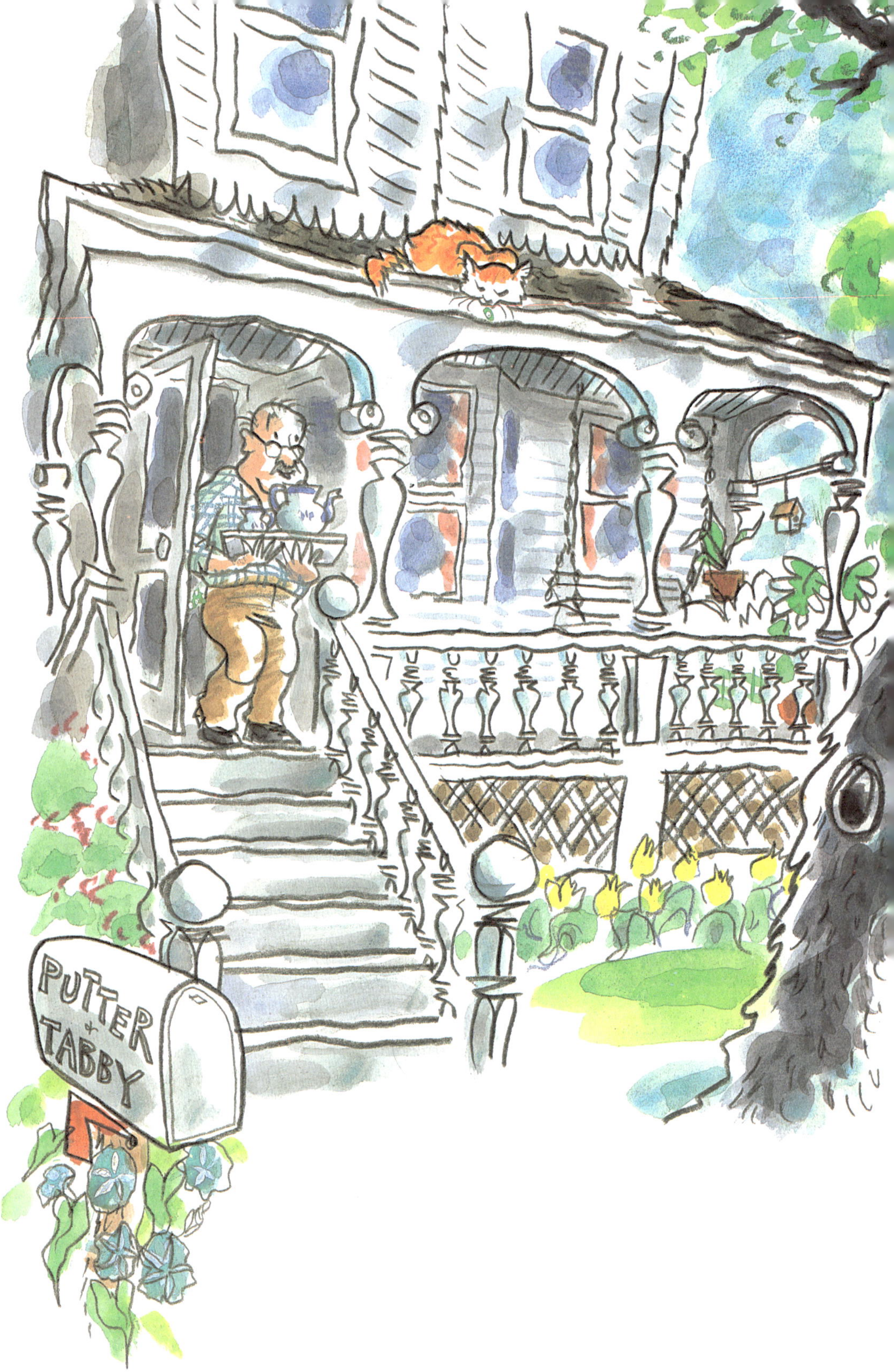
PUTTER + TABBY

Tabby could not remember
life without Mr. Putter.
They lived among their
tulips and trees.

They ate their muffins.

They poured their tea.

They turned up the opera,

and enjoyed the most perfect company of all —

each other.

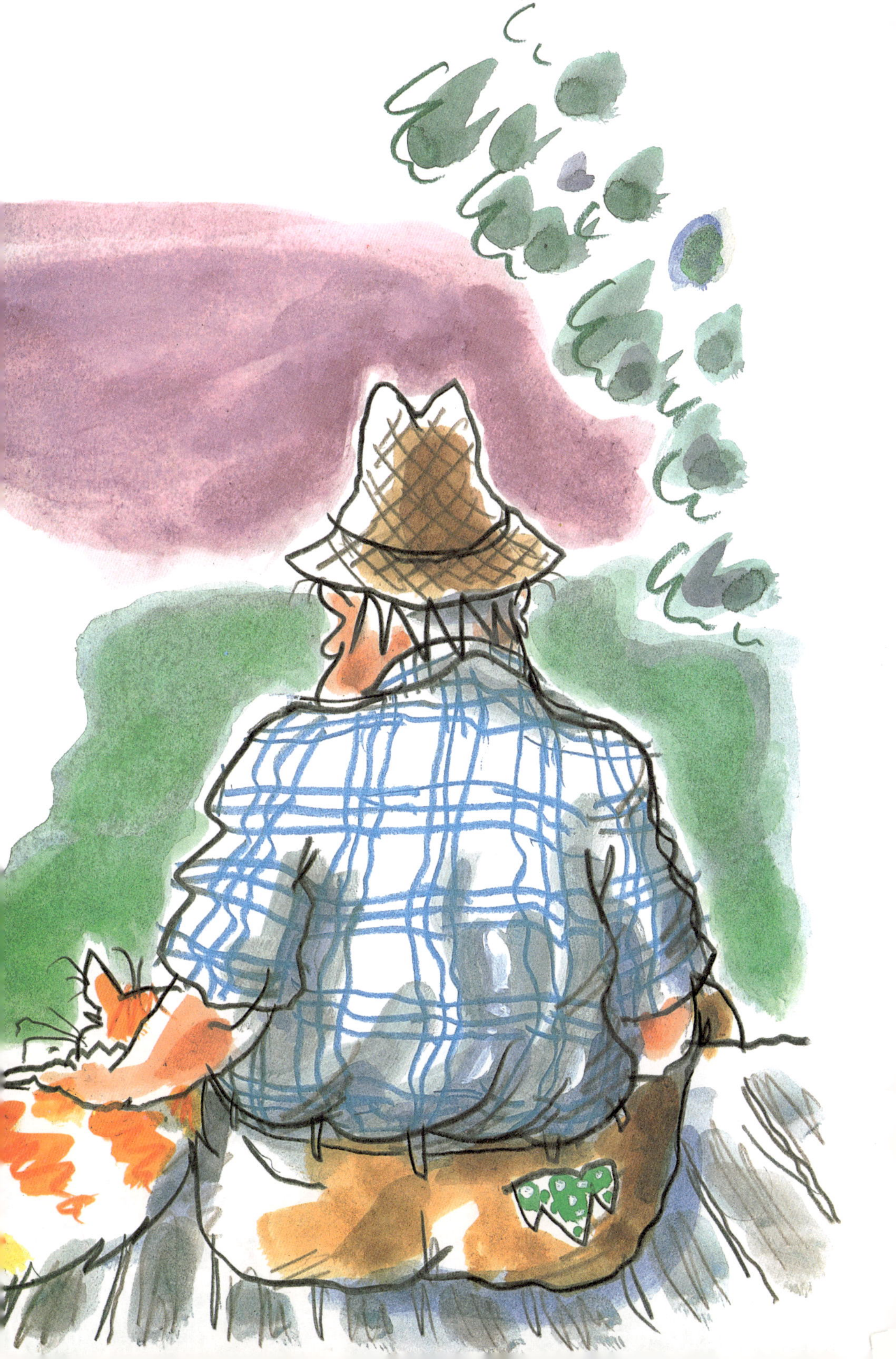

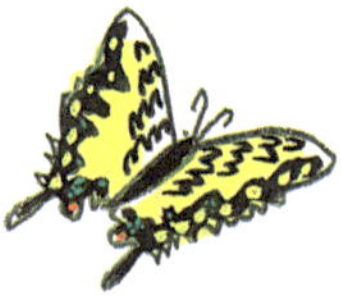
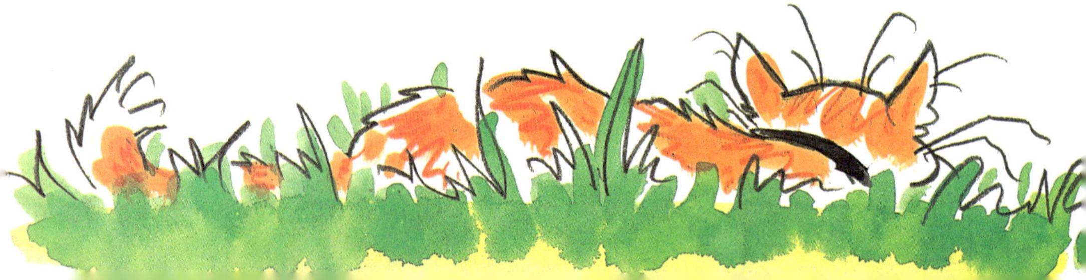